DRAGON'S Fat Cat

DRAGON'S FOURTH TALE

Dav Pilkey

SCHOLASTIC INC.

New York   Toronto   London   Auckland   Sydney

THE DRAGON TALES

ISBN 0-590-20522-6

Copyright © 1992 by Dav Pilkey.
All rights reserved.
Published by Scholastic Inc., 555 Broadway, New York, NY 10012, by arrangement
with Orchard Books.

12 11 10 9 8 7 6 5 4 3 2 1   5 6 7 8 9 0/0 9

Printed in the U.S.A.   23

First Scholastic printing, Februrary 1995

Contents

For Thrity
and her cats

One snowy day in January,
Dragon heard a funny noise.
"Meow!"
"That sounds like a cat," said Dragon.

He opened his door and looked outside.
Out in the yard, sitting in the snow,
was a fat gray cat.
"Hello, little cat," said Dragon.
"Come inside and get warm."
But the fat cat did not come inside.
The fat cat just sat in the snow and said,
"Meow."

Later, Dragon heard another funny noise.
"Meow!"
"There's that cat again," said Dragon.

"Won't you please come inside
and get warm?" Dragon asked.
But the fat cat did not come inside.
The fat cat just sat in the snow and said,
"Meow!"

The day passed, and Dragon did not hear
any more funny noises.
When Dragon looked outside,
he did not see the fat cat.
All he could see was a blanket of snow
with a fat lump in the middle.
"Oh, no!" said Dragon.
"Something is not right."

Dragon went outside
and scooped away at the snow.
He scooped and scooped and scooped
until he found the fat cat.

"You are coming with me," said Dragon.
And he took the cold cat inside.

After a few hours by the fire,
the fat cat was warm, dry, and very cozy.
The fat cat sat in Dragon's lap
and purred and purred.

"It is too cold for you
  to go back outside," said Dragon.
"So you will have to stay here with me."
  The fat cat did not seem to mind.
"And if you are going to stay with me,"
  Dragon said,
"I will have to give you a name."
  Dragon tried to think of a name
  for the fat cat.

"I will call you Cat," said Dragon.
Cat was a very good name for a cat.

"If you are going to live
  at my house," said Dragon,
"you will need a bed to sleep in."
  So Dragon took a big brown basket
  and filled it with soft blankets.
  Then he wrote Cat's name on the side.

Dragon put Cat's bed down on the floor
next to his own bed.

"How do you like your new bed?"
Dragon asked.

But Cat was already fast asleep.

And soon, so was Dragon.

3
Problems

Dragon liked living with Cat,
and Cat liked living with Dragon.
But Dragon did not know
how to take care of Cat.
He did not know how to train Cat.

That was a problem.

Dragon did not know what to feed Cat.

That was a big problem.

And Dragon did not know what to do
about all the yellow puddles Cat made.

That was a smelly problem.

Dragon tried to teach Cat to use the toilet.

But Cat did not understand.

One day the mailmouse stopped by.
"P.U.!" said the mailmouse.
"Your house stinks!"
"I know," said Dragon.
"My cat has a smelly problem."
"What you need is a litter box,"
said the mailmouse.
"A litter box will make the smelly problem
go away."
"A litter box?" said Dragon.
"That's a good idea."

So Dragon and Cat walked to the highway
and picked up all the litter
they could find.
Dragon put the litter into a box . . .

and placed the box in his house.
Now Dragon's house *really* smelled bad.
Dragon did not know what to do.
"We need to go to the pet store,"
he told Cat.

So Dragon and Cat got into the car
and drove to the pet store.

"I need to buy some cat stuff,"
 said Dragon.
"What's your cat's name?"
 asked the sales pig.
"Cat," said Dragon.
"That's a good name for a cat,"
 said the pig.
"I thought of it myself," said Dragon.

The kind old pig showed Dragon
how to take care of a cat.
She showed Dragon what to feed his cat.
And she even showed Dragon how to get
rid of the smelly problem.

Dragon bought a lot of things for Cat.
He left the pet store with everything
he needed . . .

except for one thing.

4
Left Behind

When Dragon came home,
he got his house ready for Cat.
He put out dishes of food and water.
He filled a box up with kitty litter.
And he scattered cat toys all over
the floor.

All the while, Dragon had a funny feeling.
"I feel like I've forgotten something,"
he said.

Suddenly, Dragon remembered
what he had forgotten.
"Cat!" he shouted. "I left you behind!"

Dragon found his flashlight
and went outside to look for Cat.
"Cat! Cat!" he called.
But Cat was nowhere to be found.

Dragon looked and looked
all through the night,
but he could not find Cat.

Dragon sat down on an old crate
and began to cry.
He had lost his cat.

Suddenly, Dragon heard a funny noise.
"Meow!"
Dragon looked around and around,
but he could not see Cat anywhere.
Finally, Dragon looked down
into the old crate . . .
and there was Cat.

But Cat was not alone.
Deep inside the crate,
snuggling close to Cat,
were five little kittens.
"You had babies!" said Dragon.
"Oh, you are a good cat!"

Dragon picked up the old crate
and brought it back to his warm house.

5

Home Again

Later that night, Dragon made up
good names for all of the kittens.
He then made five small beds
and wrote each kitten's name on the side.

Dragon put the kittens' beds on the
floor next to his own bed.
"How do you like your new beds?"
he asked.
But the kittens were already fast asleep.

And soon, so was Dragon.